John F. Meigs

Memoir of Charles D. Meigs

read before the College of Physicians at a stated meeting held on the 6th

of November, 1872

John F. Meigs

Memoir of Charles D. Meigs
*read before the College of Physicians at a stated meeting held on the 6th of
November, 1872*

ISBN/EAN: 9783337869786

Printed in Europe, USA, Canada, Australia, Japan

Cover: Foto ©Raphael Reischuk / pixelio.de

More available books at **www.hansebooks.com**

RESOLUTIONS

OF THE

PHILADELPHIA COLLEGE OF PHYSICIANS.

THE following resolutions, prepared by a committee, consisting of Drs. Stillé, Bell, and Coates, were adopted by the College at a stated meeting held July 7, 1869.

Resolved, That the College of Physicians have been grieved to learn of the death of their Fellow, Dr. CHARLES D. MEIGS, who had become equally venerable in character and in age, and had crowned with honor an eminent and useful career.

Resolved, That of our deceased friend it may be truly said that his heart was as warmly benevolent, and his actions as generous, as his manners were genial, kind, and winning. Zealous and conscientious in discharging his professional duties, he regarded no sacrifice of time, rest, or comfort too great when its purpose was the relief of suffering, and especially when its objects were young mothers and their tender offspring, by thousands of whom his name is blessed and will be held in grateful remembrance. Endowed with an enthusiastic love of the beautiful and true, and with a refined and delicate taste, both in nature and in art, he was not the less eager, as a scholar, to appropriate to himself the wisdom and experience of ancient times and foreign countries, for which purpose he maintained a familiarity with the classics and with several modern languages, and with equal zest enjoyed their scientific and their literary wealth. Thus copiously furnished with thought and expression, and with the fruits of an extended, varied, and well-studied experience, he naturally became a successful teacher of his favorite art, enchaining the attention of his audiences by earnestness of manner, clearness and elegance of diction, and richness of illustration, as well as by many original views in the theory and practice of medicine.

Resolved, That the personal and professional life of Dr. Meigs conspicuously illustrated the high principles which should govern a physician's conduct in his relations to his brethren, his patients, and society, and may be safely appealed to as an example and a guide.

Resolved, That a copy of these resolutions, properly attested, be communicated to the family of Dr. Meigs.

In accordance with a further resolution of the College, Dr. JOHN FORSYTH MEIGS was appointed to prepare a biographical memoir of their deceased Fellow.

MEMOIR

CHARLES D. MEIGS, M.D.

READ BEFORE THE COLLEGE OF PHYSICIANS AT A STATED MEETING
HELD ON THE 6TH OF NOVEMBER, 1872.

By J. F. MEIGS, M.D.

FELLOWS OF THE COLLEGE OF PHYSICIANS OF PHILADELPHIA.

GENTLEMEN: When I accepted the request of the College, made through its proper officers, to prepare for its archives a biographical sketch of its late member, my father, Dr. Chas. D. Meigs, I did so with much diffidence.

I feared my relationship might warp my judgment, and my filial love exaggerate his merits. But who could know him as I knew him? Not only did I pass all the usual time which a son, reared at home, spends under the paternal roof, but, under the power of a great misfortune which occurred to myself, after having been separated from him for the period of twelve years, I again took up my abode with him during, with very few interruptions, the remainder of his life. Not only this. We were of the same profession. Our interests, moral, intellectual, social, and economical, were linked together. The same subjects interested us equally, and I came to know him, or ought to have known him, better than any ordinary or professional acquaintance could have done—better than most sons can know their fathers.

Should I, in the notice of his life, which I am about to read, portray his virtues too highly, or his defects too lightly, I must beg you to excuse me for the reason that he was my father.

I desire to state, also, that portions of this sketch were prepared by my son, Mr. Harry I. Meigs.

I suppose I am not different from other men, and being myself always anxious to know from whence men of mark have come, and under what conditions they may have developed, I assume that others have the same taste, and I shall, therefore, dwell at greater length upon my father's family, and upon the circumstances connected with his early life, than is always done in these formal sketches.

I will speak of his family at the risk of being prolix, for I could not paint his true character without referring to his progenitors. He was

1

fond of his genealogical tree, though it was not a very tall one, but he insisted that it was most respectable, and that it was the duty of all men, when they could, to teach their children their family history, and to place before them the rigid duty incumbent upon them, to do whatever might be in their power to promote its honorableness before men. Many a warning did my brothers and I receive from him not to disgrace the stock from which we had come. I believe firmly that these appeals from him, this faith he had in the honor and respectability of his ancestors, had a positive influence upon his own children, in lending them a motive towards uprightness in their walk through life. That such teachings are not more common in our young country is, I think, a misfortune. Not that he ever taught us that a man should rest his own foundations on mere traits of family history, but that he should beware lest he disgraced that history.

At the end of his family Bible, he wrote, on the 25th March, 1862, at Hamanassett, his country seat, a note addressed to his children, in which he says: "My desire is that you should carefully preserve, each one of you, the record of our family.

"If all men could be induced to preserve their family records, discarding without mercy every member of their blood-line whose conduct might stain it, society would derive great security, and virtue a strong support from that course.

"If it should be deemed unfair to ignore discreditable members of a line, then at least let a mark of disapprobation be set opposite their record."

It was in this way that he spoke to his children all through his life, and it must have been in the blood, for I happen to know that my grandfather and my great uncle felt and wrote in the same style. It was an inherited trait. Habit, says Darwin, is omnipotent, and its effects hereditary, and how do we know that the wise and virtuous life of my father may not have been in part the result of such opinions firmly held by those who had gone before him, and by them transmitted to him?

My father came, on both sides of the house, from a New England stock, people of very moderate possessions as to worldly goods, who earned, as farmers, the means of living from the cold soil of Connecticut, or who, as small manufacturers, and sometimes, as I have reason to believe, as hatters, were well inured to daily labor, and to habits of simplicity and economy. They were people of strong natures, bringing into the world large families, receiving them with thankfulness and without fear, and rearing them in habits of honest industry. They were patient, too, and submissive to the decrees of Providence, as witness the conduct of my father's great grandfather, Janna Meigs, who, amongst nine children, had twins born to him on the 5th January, 1711, and who named them Silence and Submit. The story goes, that on the announcement of the arrival of the first, to check the rejoicing of the family, he said "Silence;" and on that of the second, moved by his patient spirit, he said, "Submit." The twins afterwards were given these names.

My father was the fifth of ten children born to Josiah Meigs. Josiah Meigs was in the sixth generation from Vincent Meigs, who came to this country from Dorsetshire, England, with his son John, and settled in East Guilford, Connecticut, about 1647 or 1648. This Vincent Meigs died in East Guilford in 1658. From Vincent Meigs down to my grandfather, my father's direct ancestors adhered to the flinty soil of New England, and lived their lives, such as they were, surrounded by and fully blended with the political, social, and religious faith of those days. A story is told of one of them who was dealt with by the authorities of the day, for breaking the Sabbath, in a way which would seem, in these times, the most besotted rigor and fanaticism. I found the account in a letter to my grandfather, from a Mr. Lee, of East Guilford, 7th April, 1816. It was shown me by Mr. R. J. Meigs, of Washington.

This gentleman sends a copy of the proceedings of the court as follows : " At a regular court held at Guilford, December 4th, 1657, John Meggs being called for on a complaint, that he came with his cart from Hamanassett late in the night on the Lord's day, making a noise, as he came, to the offence of many who heard it, then appeared and answered, that he was mistaken in the time of the day, thinking that he had had time enough for the journey. But being somewhat more laden than he apprehended, the cattle came more slowly than usual, and so cast him behind, it proving to be more late of the day than he had thought. But he professeth to be sorry for his mistake and the offence justly given thereby, promising to be more careful for the time to come.

" The court considering the premises did see cause (seeing that the matter seemed to be done through a surprisall, and not wittingly) to pass it over with a reproof for this first time, on his giving a public acknowledgment of his evil in so neglecting to remember the Sabbath, on the next lecture or fast day, with all the aggravating circumstances in it.

Signed, WILLIAM LEETE."

This Wm. Leete was governor of the colony of New Haven, and after the colonies of New Haven and Hartford had been united, was governor of the State, and there is no doubt he was a true Republican, for he secreted for some time three of Oliver Cromwell's generals—Goff, Dixwell, and Whalley.

My grandfather, Josiah Meigs, was the thirteenth child of his mother, and was born in the 49th year of her age. He married Clara Benjamin, of Stratford, Connecticut, January 21st, 1782. This lady, my grandmother, was descended from John Benjamin, who settled at Watertown, Massachusetts, in 1632, and died there June, 1645. Her father was Col. John Benjamin, who lived at Stratford, Conn., 1731, and died there in 1796, partly from a bullet wound received at the battle of Ridgefield in the Revolutionary war. This gentleman had named his youngest son Charles Delucena, after a Spanish gentleman to whom he had become strongly attached during the war. My father's name was given him in remembrance of this uncle.

Amongst some notes in regard to the family, left by my father, I find the following account of my grandfather. He says : " My father, Josiah Meigs, a native of Middletown, in Connecticut, was the son of Return Meigs of the same city. . . . . My father was educated at Yale College, after having labored in his father's (Return) vocation (a hatter) for a few of his early years. He was an excellent Greek and Latin and French scholar, and made high attainments in mathematics. He cultivated with some success a love for the sciences of botany and geology, and as a general litterateur and scholar had few superiors, so that, take him all in all, it will be rare to meet with a person of more extensive and diversified knowledge than was possessed by that gentle and good man." After his marriage he went, somewhere about 1789 or 1790, to St. George's, Bermuda, to practice as a proctor in the courts of admiralty. He soon became tired of this work, and longing for his native country, returned and settled in New Haven, where he was soon after elected professor of mathematics and natural philosophy at Yale College.

He was a man of fine culture, and was always longing to be amongst his books. Years after he had left Yale College and the Georgia University, and when he was General Land Commissioner in the city of Washington, I may mention, to show his general interest in scientific matters, he endeavored to establish in Washington a system of meteorological observations, which might well have been the foundation of the present bureau. In 1817, as he wrote to Dr. Drake, of Cincinnati, he had applied to the national legislature for authority to make it the duty of the various land agents under him to take observations on temperature, pressure, rain, wind, etc., and suggested Detroit, St. Louis, Opelousas, St. Stephen, etc. etc., as points to begin with. He also asked for a small appropriation for the purchase of the necessary instruments. He says in one of his letters : "Without some system of this kind, our country may be occupied for ages, and we, the people of the United States, be as ignorant on this subject as the Kickapoos now are, who have occupied a part of it for ages past."

My father's early years were passed under very different circumstances from those which have attended the lives of most of the fellows of this college; and if the words of the great philosophic poet, "the child is father to the man," be true, the days of childhood must have much to do with a man's after years, and the college will not, I hope, think me tedious or unwisely prolix if I tell here some of the particular circumstances under which he grew up.

He was born in the island of St. George's, one of the group of the Bermudas. If we suppose that, even in infancy, impressions are made on the soul never to be effaced, we can well imagine that the scenes amidst which he was born, and where he passed the earliest period of his life, had something to do with the large imaginative faculty he exhibited through his life. "Nothing," says a writer who was well acquainted with St. George's, "can be more romantic than the little bay of St. George's ; the number of little islets, the singular clearness of the water, and the animated play of the graceful little boats gliding between the islands and seeming to sail from one cedar grove to another, form altogether the sweetest miniature of nature that can be imagined. In the short but beautiful twilight of their summer evenings, the white cottages scattered over the islands, and but partially seen through the trees that surround them, assume often the appearance of Grecian temples, and embellish the poor fisherman's hut with colors which the pencil of Claude might imitate."

My father was born on the 19th of February, 1792. I have already said that my grandfather had gone to St. George's to practice as a proctor in the English courts of admiralty. They remained there until May, 1796.

From this beautiful southern home he was taken to the ruder climate, and to the very different atmosphere, intellectual, social, and religious, of New England. My grandfather was made professor of mathematics and astronomy at Yale College, and under the shade of that college at New Haven my father passed the period of life between two and nine years of age.

The domestic and social atmosphere of a small town in New England, the seat of a great school of learning, with the added influences belonging to the household of a professor of mathematics, must have had great influence in the formation of his moral and mental character. Here he must have imbibed much of that strong sense of duty which he carried through life. Honesty, honor, love of country, inflexible uprightness, liberality of mind, and love of knowledge were here implanted in him. His father, a student always, and a teacher; his home the seat of scholarship and of moderation. No love of money for money's sake. I cannot but think that these early associations had much to do with that thirst for knowledge, that love of science and literature, which he exhibited to the very last day of his life.

In 1801, when my father was eight years old, the family left the cold north for the warm south again, and he was now removed to the air and moral atmosphere of the State of Georgia. At Athens, a little town in Clarke County, Georgia, within twenty-eight miles of the border, beyond which still roamed the tribes of the Cherokee and Creek Indians, was to be built up a new institution of learning, the University of Georgia, and my father was to see the very birth and growth of the college which was to be his Alma Mater, and where he was to acquire that knowledge of the classics, of the severe sciences, and of the French language, which was to aid him in the strife of a long and arduous professional career.

Clarke County, Georgia, in which Athens is situated, is a healthy, but not a fertile region. At the time when my grandfather removed there it was a wild place, and but thinly populated. I could not find the population in the census of 1800, but in that of 1810 the population of the county is set down at 7628, and that of the town at 273; of these latter 95 were white males, 40 free white females, 134 slaves, and all other free persons, except Indians, not taxed, 4.

The family, except my grandfather, remained for some time in Augusta, whilst he proceeded to Athens to superintend the erection of the college buildings, and also of a house for himself. In a letter dated Athens, but without other date, to his brother, Col. Return Jonathan Meigs, then Indian Agent at Hiawassee, in Tennessee, he says: " I arrived at this place two days ago. Here is the seat of the University of Georgia, over which I preside. We are making bricks for a large college building, 120 feet long, 45 wide, and three stories high. We have plenty of timber all around us, and thus far everything looks very favorable to the completion of the building. Our great difficulty is the procuring of lime. This part of the country affords no limestone." This was in 1801, for there is another letter, dated Athens, Sept. 25th, 1801, in which he thanks his brother for his attention to the limestone, though he does not say whether he obtained any or not. It appears from White's Georgia, published at Savannah, in 1849, that liberal endowments had been made to the Franklin College or University of Georgia, as early as 1788, but that it did not go into operation until 1801.

So that my father, having first seen the light under the soft summer sun of the Bermudas, having then been removed to the cold New England climate, where he passed seven years under the very shadow and protection of one of the greatest learned institutions of the day, now found himself at a little frontier town, whose population numbered only two hundred and seventy-three souls, in a slave instead of a free State, where he was to witness the laying of the foundation stones and the building up of the walls of a new institution of learning. Here, in this little village, in a semi-wild, sparsely-inhabited country, rolling in character, elevated, healthy, with great forests all around, a beautiful, rapid river—the Oconee—close by, was he to spend the latter years of his boyhood. Within twenty-eight miles of him was a country still occupied by the native Indian—the various tribes of the Cherokees, Creeks, Choctaws, and Chickasaws—and but a short distance from this near frontier, at Hiawassee, in Tennessee, lived his uncle, Col. R. J. Meigs, his father's elder and best-beloved brother, who at this time, and for many years after, was the government Indian agent, having these tribes in his care. This gallant gentleman had fought all through the Revolutionary war, had received a sword from Congress for gallant conduct on Long Island. He had accompanied Arnold to Quebec, and there been taken prisoner, and had led one of the storming parties at Stony Point under Wayne. He must have been a man of rare qualities. He was over six feet in height, and at eighty-two years of age walked with the step of a young man, erect as a tree, and light and free. His character was such that his brother always speaks of him in his letters with an almost reverent affection and admiration. He was called by the Indians, whom he so long watched over, the White Chief.

It must have been a curious admixture of law and lawlessness, of wild nature and cultivated humanity, of education and refinement, and of ignorance and downright barbarism, in which my father now found himself placed. In the centre the little town of two hundred and seventy-three inhabitants, with its new collegiate buildings slowly lifting themselves from the rude soil on which they had but just been planted; around the town, no doubt, some few cultivated fields; the river running fresh and sparkling from the mountains to the north and west; and, only a few miles off, the wild native forest, as yet untouched by the hand of man. Here was a spot, a climate—forest and stream, hill and dale—well calculated to tempt a hardy, active, and most restless child to the pursuits best fitted to develop a strong and vigorous body, to train the eye and ear, and, indeed all the perceptive faculties which are so much needed for the acquisition of all knowledge, and especially of the arts of human life. Not only so, but the basis of that decision of character, which, under the various terms of courage, pluck, grit, endurance, constitutes, it seems to me, the chiefest element in the mental constitution of most of our ablest and most successful men—that predominance of will which comes of a sound, robust body, and which we ought all to endeavor to evolve in our children—must have here been laid in my father, broad and deep.

But not only were the outer scenes, in which he was now to live, calculated to develop robustness of body and mind, but the circumstances of the family were such as to promote the wholesome virtues of economy, patience, and sobriety in all things. What his father's income might have been from the college endowments I know not, but it must have been small, for the household was generally but poorly supplied with money, and at times had so little that it may well have looked forward with anxiety as to the supplies for the next day, as will be shown by a story my father was very fond of telling—to his children first, and to his grandchildren afterwards.

My son tells the story as he heard it often from his grandfather's lips. "My grandfather's father was a professor of mathematics in one of our Northern universities, and like many distinguished wits of a hundred years ago was always out of money, not from any bad habit of borrowing or lending, but from the very flow of charity that welled forth in his big heart toward all who were in need. Though a strict Presbyterian himself, the catholic doctrine of good works was the very corner-stone of his creed, and of him it might literally be said that, if a man asked him for his coat, he gave him his cloak also. One day, in Athens, my grandfather, who was then called Charlie, saw a man on the bank of the Oconee, with such a big fish that its equal had never been known in those parts, and the simple people thought it must have been raised by magic, or that the day of judgment was come, which, indeed, is the commonest way for our country people to understand anything unusual. My grandfather at once had an eager wish to become the possessor of it, and he ran to his mother, and begged her to give him a dollar, which was the price of the curiosity. 'My son,' said she, 'there is but twice what you ask for in the house, and would you take the half of all that I have?' But the boy's thoughts were full of the fish, and he could not listen to moral philosophy. So his mother, being a woman of great generosity, and seeing that remonstrance was vain, gave him what he asked for in the shape of one of those clumsy silver dollars that have now passed entirely out of use. Charlie put it into his pocket, and ran down to the river; but, as he went swinging his jacket round his head like a sling, it is no wonder that when he reached the bottom of the hill, what with the centrifugal force of the jacket and the force of gravity of the coin, the dollar was gone, and he found himself as poor as when he first coveted the fish. For an instant he was in terrible grief, but quickly the buoyancy of his mind overcame all sadness, and he ran back again to his mother, to ask for the remaining dollar. The good woman had by this time caught some of her son's fire, and with scarce a murmur she gave him what was left of her estate, thinking perhaps, in her simplicity, that, if the fish was really so great, it might serve the whole family for food until a fresh instalment should be paid to the worthy President."

But not only did my father have the advantages of the healthy climate and simple habits of this little village, where learning and refinement were so curiously blended with the rude nature around, and with the people that made up its small population; he became familiar with many of the phases of a truly savage life. He had made the acquaintance of a certain Jim Vann, a well-known and conspicuous Indian of the Cherokee tribe, who had a store on the frontier, twenty-eight miles from Athens, and who often passed through Athens on his way to or from Savannah to make purchases and carry his goods home. On one occasion, when on his way down to the coast, he said to my father, "Now, Charley, if your mother will let you, I will take you back to the Indian country when I return, where you can see how we live, and I will give you the finest Indian (Injin) pony in the country." How often have I heard him describe his delight at this offer and promise! Vann was to be absent several weeks, and during these weeks my father laid such diligent siege to his mother that, though at first she flatly and with high indignation refused even to listen to such a project, he never ceased to beg and entreat, and knock, until finally, in very despair of escape from his knockings, she yielded, and it was agreed that when Vann returned he should be allowed to go with him. And so it happened that after waiting long for Vann's return, until hope almost died out, he found himself one day in the early part of January, 1805, mounted behind the Indian on a powerful black horse on his journey to visit these natives in their own country, and to live for a while amongst them in their own ways. I fix the date accurately, for I find, in a letter from my grandfather to his brother, dated Athens, February 11th, 1805, this passage: "Charles is now in the Nation, as I suppose. He went from us about a month ago in company with J. Vann, who promised to give him a horse. I expect him in a few days." The Nation must have been in a very quiet and orderly state, or he would scarcely have written in this cool way about his son, then not quite thirteen years old, who had left his home en croupe behind an Indian, known to be a most violent and brutal fellow in some moods, though generous and kind in others. Only four years later I find him writing again to his brother, April 23d, 1809, as follows: "Poor Vann has *ceased from troubling*, and the circumstance must be pleasing to you, for his death was a public blessing."

When I read this last passage of my grandfather's letter, about Jim Vann, which I did only this year in Washington, where I found a collection of his letters, I could not but think of the time when I, as a boy, used to listen open-mouthed to my father's accounts of his expedition with Jim Vann. As I grew older, I came to think that some of his stories about Vann's savagery and wildness must have been exaggerations, but when I found my grandfather writing to his brother, the government agent to the very tribe to which Vann belonged, that his death must be pleasing to him, and that it was a public blessing, I can well believe that all my father's stories may have been quite within the truth.

The Indian fulfilled his promise and gave the boy an Indian pony which he brought home with him. This pony was for years his most precious possession, and its speed, easy gaits, intelligence, docility, and hardiness, were described first to his own children, and then to his grandchildren, with a picturesque minuteness, which forever stamped the image of the gallant little horse on their minds.

From this time, 1805 to 1809, he resided with his parents in Athens, going on regularly with his various classical and English studies in the Franklin College. What kind of a faculty they may have had I do not know, but I do know that here was laid for him a foundation of classical knowledge which he never lost, and a thirst for learning which he carried literally to the last day of his life. The college must have begun its career in a very simple style, as he says in a very short sketch which he left of his early years, that when they moved to Georgia, his father found but three or four houses in Athens on arriving there, and that they erected a wooden hut which served as recitation room and chapel.

The dwelling-house which the president occupied, and which was prepared for him by the trustees, was seated on the brow of a considerable hill, and consisted of a frame building of the plainest kind. It had a basement story first, apparently not below the level of the ground, a second story, and an attic. The main story was reached by steps from the yard, and these steps ascended to a piazza or veranda, running the whole front of the house, the roof of which piazza consisted of an extension of the roof of the house. At the gable ends were brick or clay chimneys. The house was low and very plain, and could not have had many rooms in it, so that where they bestowed all the children, and yet gave the president any room to himself, I cannot imagine.

In the little sketch of his early life I referred to just now, he says: "After getting settled at the house of the President of the University of Georgia, for such was my father's qualification, I began at the grammar school, which was soon set on foot, and here I learned my *penna*, a pen, and *regnum*, a kingdom, and even made a beginning in the Tupto and

Agapo, a dreadful labor to a child who would have much preferred to wade in Hall's branch, or stand on the river's bank and see the water as it flashed and boiled amongst the rocks of the shoals of Oconee hard by at the bottom of the hill."

Here is another passage describing his early life in Athens. "Thus in the wild woods of Georgia, by the perseverance of my worthy father, were the blessings of literature and philosophy begun to be scattered abroad in a new country—close by the frontiers of the savage Creek and the gallant Cherokee. The high sounding song of Homer, the sweet notes of Virgil, the stirring narratives of Xenophon and Cæsar, the denunciations, the suasion, and the arguments of Tully, heard no more in the native land of the philosopher, were familiar sounds on the air of Athens. And many was the boy who got under his kind and patient and wise teachings clear views of Kepler's laws, and they knew the risings of the Pleiades and all the gems of Orion's belt and the whole train of Ophiuchus huge. There were taught geometry, trigonometry, and conic sections. There we made beautiful projections of eclipses a thousand years overpassed and a thousand to come, and we painted the bright sun with gamboge to show how yellow his light is, and the shadow of the earth was a great cone of India ink, and the orbit of the earth was Prussian blue. These magnificent results of art were formed on sheets of paper pasted together to make one vast sheet, and hung up in the Philosophical Hall, where we had a telescope, an air-pump, and several other things to study and practice astronomy withal."

In Athens my father had the good fortune to find a professor of the French language, Petit de Clairviere, an intelligent and cultivated *emigré*, with whom he was very intimate, and with whom, indeed, I believe he lived a good deal. From this gentleman he gained a really fine French accent early in life, and an acquaintance with the language so full, that I have heard his French patients in Philadelphia declare that they knew no man that had not been in France, speak the language as well as he did. I can well believe, too, that he may have acquired from this gentleman some of the gentle and courteous manner which he had throughout his long professional career.

He graduated at the University of Georgia in 1809, as I learn from a catalogue of the institution which was kindly sent me by A. A. Lipscomb, D.D., the present chancellor. After his graduation he began the study of medicine in 1809. He says himself that he began his studies under the roof of Dr. Thomas Hanson Marshall Fendall, to whom he became apprenticed. I believe this was in Augusta, and I suppose he may have had his board and lodging for his services. He says (in one of his lectures or sketches) that he lived three long years under the roof of his master, Dr. Fendall, and then went home. This must have been in 1812. I do not know what home this could have been but that of his sister, Mrs. John Forsyth, in Augusta. His father had resigned his presidency in 1811 and removed to Cincinnati, where he remained until 1814.

During his stay with Dr. Fendall he served as apothecary boy as well as medical apprentice, for I have often heard him laugh over his pestle and mortar experiences, and especially his manufacture of a certain plaster, of which he used to make, with long suffering watchfulness, and stirrings, great quantities. He was often sent out by his master to apply blisters, to cup, leech, bleed, and perform the various ministrations which the sick constantly need.

He attended, after leaving Dr. Fendall, two courses of medicine in the University of Pennsylvania, the first in 1812–13, and the second in 1814–15, according to my friend Prof. Carson.

I may mention, to show the difficulties he had to contend with, that he borrowed money to pay for his tickets and for the other expenses attendant upon his trip to the North. Some of these debts were paid after his marriage. Not that they were paid out of his wife's property. That was unnecessary, since he had a very good practice when he settled in Augusta, immediately after his marriage.

He states in one of his manuscript lectures, that he got one course of lectures at the University of Pennsylvania, and "then went home to set up for myself, and practice on that stock in trade. I was still lamentably ignorant of all save some methods. I was twenty-one years of age, and assumed to be a physician!! Everybody called me doctor; I thought so myself." This must have been in 1813, two years before his marriage.

I found from the minutes of the Trustees of the University of Pennsylvania, under the date of April 10th, 1817, that he was graduated at a commencement held in that year, though he was at that time still in Georgia. His name is given in the catalogue of graduates as being from South Carolina. The name of his preceptor is not given. The subject of his thesis was Prolapsus Uteri.

It was in Philadelphia, in the winter of 1814–15, whilst attending lectures, that my father met with the great good fortune of his life, in making the acquaintance of my mother. He had a letter from one of the large cotton merchants of Augusta to my grandfather, Mr. Wm. Montgomery, then a prominent and active merchant in this city. He delivered the letter, but made no intimate acquaintance with the family at first. Upon what slight chances do the fortunes of men often hang! My father took a whim one day to have a sail up the Delaware River, in one of the little sloops which then formed the means of water transport between this city and Burlington, Bristol, and Bordentown. On that very day, as it chanced, my mother and her sister were to go up the river to Bordentown, to pay a visit. On reaching the wharf to embark, their escort, by some accident, failed them. My grandfather, embarrassed to know what to do, suddenly espied my father on the wharf, about to go on board of the sloop. On seeing him, and finding that he was going up the river, he soon settled the matter. "Why, girls, here is Mr. Meigs, who is to be your fellow-passenger; he will take care of you." And so agreeable and engaging did he prove in his care, that on that day was laid the foundation of my father's greatest happiness in life, for there he learned to value my mother for what she was, and there began that attachment which was to end only with his life.

I will not detain you with any account of my mother's family, except only so much as to show what manner of woman my father was drawn towards. Her name was Montgomery, and, on her father's side, she came of the Montgomerys of Ayreshire, Scotland, who carry their generations, according to history, far back into the past. She was worthy of any race, for she was just, true, faithful, devoted, and during my father's long and arduous battle with a large and most responsible obstetric practice in a large city, she never failed to make his home the home of virtue and moderation and calm. She bore him ten children, nursed them all herself, and was so faithful to them throughout, that, though several had most violent and prolonged attacks of illness during infancy and childhood, but one was wrested from her hands. Nine of those children live to this day to bear witness to the goodness, and justice, and devotion of the woman, who married in 1815 the young doctor from the far South (then called a Varginny student), whom, though without other fortune than his talents and fine character, she read truly as one to whom a noble woman might indeed be the crown and jewel of a wife.

They were married in Philadelphia, March 15th, 1815, at the close of the lectures. Dr. Jacob Randolph was one of the groomsmen. Soon after their marriage they sailed for the South, where my father was to go regularly into practice in Augusta, Georgia, in partnership, I believe, with a Dr. Cunningham. They reached Augusta safely, where they remained until the summer of 1817.

During this time my father had quite a large business, became popular, and was successful. I found amongst my grandfather's letters, one written from Washington, March 4th, 1816, to Dr. Drake, of Cincinnati, but just then in Philadelphia, in which he says: " There is some alarm here on account of a malady of the nature of Peripneumony. The Esculapii here appear not to have settled the question of the treatment. How true it is that a physician ought to be *vere Physicus*, a naturalist—master of nature. The diseases of particular positions vary, perhaps, as much as religious opinions. I do not believe that a man or a family educated in Norway, or in New England, in the severe habits of Calvinism, would, if transported to the vale of Arcadia, retain all the rigidity of the Reformer of Geneva. My son Charles, who is a physician at Augusta, Georgia, tells me (Feb. 18th, 1816), that the diseases there 'are most exceedingly sthenic, so much so, that I have been frequently compelled to bleed four, six, eight, and once thirteen times. Now, it is not more than sixty miles direct from this to Columbia, South Carolina, where, I am credibly informed, that the constitution of the atmosphere is so asthenic that one bleeding often is sufficient to produce death.' This, if true," comments my grandfather, " is very curious." Well might he say it was very curious, if true.

After residing a year and a half at Augusta, during which time my father had more than one attack of bilious fever, and my mother had been greatly shocked by some of the scenes incident to the slavery system, my father determined to remove permanently to the North, and to seek his fortune there instead of in the scenes of his youth. And happy was it for him, and I may safely say, for medical science and for his children, that he carried out, with a resolute spirit, this removal.

He left Georgia in 1817, as I know accurately from a letter of my grandfather, who writes to Dr. Drake from Washington, June 13th, 1817. " My son, the doctor, will, I trust, be a useful citizen in his profession. He has left Georgia to reside in Philadelphia, where, through the assistance and influence of his father-in-law, I think he will be able to establish himself advantageously. He pursues the sciences relative to his profession *con amore*, with ardor and enthusiasm. He is a truly worthy and excellent young man. This you will believe, though his father says it.

" He sailed from Charleston, S. C., on the 5th of the month, and in *three* days arrived in New York! We knew he was to sail at that time, and as *we* had a *northeast* storm at that period, we predicted for him a boisterous and tedious passage, but he writes me that from Charleston the ship was immediately placed eastward of the Gulf Stream, and took a *southeast* current of atmosphere which drove them like an arrow from the bow, through the whole transit, without variation of force or direction. This is a curious meteorological fact." This letter was written about the time that he was discussing with Drake his plan for having careful and extended meteorological observations for the whole country.

When the family reached Philadelphia they settled in a small house in Eighth Street above Race, on the west side, where they lived until after the death of my grandmother, when they removed to my grandfather Montgomery's house, in Arch Street above Sixth.

He obtained practice only very slowly, the position of his wife's family in society doing him no more good than to convey to a certain moderate circle of people the information that there had arrived in the city another aspirant for employment in the medical profession. As usual his wife's relatives did not, and indeed they could not, be expected to employ him in so delicate a position as that of physician, until he had in some measure shown himself fit to be so trusted. Gradually, however, business came to him; first, the poor and destitute, and then slowly those in better circumstances.

In the meantime he studied his profession and belles-lettres. He soon joined the Medical Society of Philadelphia, and was a very active and useful member. He took part in many of the discussions, and showed the members of his own profession what manner of man he was. He soon became intimate with Drs. La Roche, Hodge, Bond, Coates, Wood, Bache, and Bell.[1]

Dr. George B. Wood, in his very interesting "Biographical Memoir of Dr. Franklin Bache," read before this College, May 3d, and January 7th, 1865, states that my father began to lecture on midwifery in what was called the School of Medicine in 1830, and continued to do this for some five or six years.

He was also one of the first editors of the *North American Medical and Surgical Journal*, the first number of which appeared in 1826, and the last in October, 1831. This journal, Dr. Wood states, was started by the Kappa Lambda Society of this city, in order to promote its ends, and was edited by a committee of its members—Drs. La Roche, H. L. Hodge, F. Bache, C. D. Meigs, and B. Hornor Coates. On the appearance of the seventh number of the Journal there were added to the above Dr. John Bell, Dr. D. F. Condie, and Dr. G. B. Wood. These gentlemen, however, whose names now first appeared in the Journal, had co-operated with the previous committee from the beginning.

Besides these occupations he was a busy reader in many different directions. He devoured books with great ardor and rapidity. But even with these literary occupations he had, owing to his small practice, a good many unoccupied hours, and some of these he passed in a workshop he had arranged in the garret of his house. In this room was a very fine lathe which he had bought of Isaiah Lukens, one of the most noted scientific mechanicians of the day, and with whom he had become quite intimately associated in a mutual liking and friendship. Here he turned in metal and wood. Well do I recollect, when I could not have been more than six or seven years of age, seeing him hurry down stairs from the garret to the office, brushing as he went with his hands the dust and shavings from his vest and pants. I can see him now,

[1] He was elected a Fellow of the College of Physicians in 1827; was one of its Censors from 1841 to 1848; and was Vice-President from 1848 to 1855.

as I recall those days, going rapidly down the staircase, with clouds of dust, wood parings, and chips floating after him as a trail. He had a carpenter's bench, too, with planes and saws, and all the paraphernalia of a carpenter's business. There was a beautiful little blacksmith's bellows, with a small iron furnace, an anvil, and a veritable sledge, all of which were objects of the most passionate admiration of myself and brothers.

Not content with the pursuits I have mentioned he drew, and tried his hand at painting, both in oils and water-colors. And it was not mere daubing in his case, for he had a fine artistic faculty, and could draw and color with very considerable skill. One of his portraits in oil, of an old nurse, one of those faithful women who had nursed my mother when a child and her children afterwards, was an excellent likeness.

Let not any one suppose that the time passed by him in these pursuits was lost time. Not so. The mind wearies and dulls when applied too persistently to one object of study ; and it was wise in my father at this period of his life, when his practice was growing so slowly, to spend a portion of his time in the cultivation of his perceptive faculties. There can be no doubt that the free and easy use of these faculties which he thus obtained, was of great use to him in after life, when he was compelled to determine, by touch alone, the conditions of the patient and child in the lying-in-room, and to use instruments without the aid of the eye. He was the best nurse I ever saw, and could handle and move an ill woman, or a little frail, new-born child, with a grace, ease, and precision I never saw equalled. In after life, when a teacher of obstetrics, his knowledge of drawing enabled him to make diagrams and paintings with which to illustrate his lectures.

In addition to drawing and painting he tried his hand at modelling in clay and wax, and, when the time came, was ready to make models of those materials with which to teach the medical student many of the difficult anatomical, physiological, and operative portions of his art.

May I not say that I think the younger men in the profession might well take example after him in some such course as this ? Had he not had these tastes and cultivated them, he might have passed the hours not devoted to study alone in mere useless society, in dawdling, in smoking, or worse, in the formation of some habits of dissipation.

As time went on his practice increased slowly, but steadily. And now I shall mention a curious episode in his career, which may be reassuring to others in the future, and which shows what slaves to circumstances men often are. He had, in his early life, his average share of obstetrical practice, and then, as afterwards, as much success as others. He chanced, however, to have, at a certain period of time, several very difficult cases of child-birth, which greatly disturbed and tried his strength and nerves. In one of these he made a wrong diagnosis, and though no harm came of the mistake either to mother or child, he was so disgusted with himself for the error, and with the painful responsibility belonging to that branch, that he resolved to avoid it for the future, and for two years sent all such cases to one of his friends. But he soon found that he made small headway in practice without obstetrics, and seeing his family growing, his expenses increasing, his years accumulating, he began to fancy that the wolf was approaching his door, and, for the sake of his family, he resumed obstetrics, and from that day went ever on with increasing business and reputation, until he had achieved the main duty of life—an honorable support for his family, the education of his children, and their establishment in positions for themselves.

Besides the pursuits I have already alluded to, he was interested in general scientific matters. I find him writing to his uncle, Col. R. J. Meigs, the Indian agent, from Philadelphia, of the date of December 19th, 1820: "My dear uncle. I am exceedingly anxious to possess the skull of a Cherokee, a Choctaw, or Creek, or indeed of any other *pure* aboriginal inhabitant of the United States. I know no one to whom I can apply with a prospect of success like yourself; and, if you could oblige me, I should feel very grateful for it, while I should set much value on its acquisition.

"We are told that 50 or 60 years ago many of the Choctaws had their heads flattened by a peculiar process. I would be more gratified by the acquirement of such a skull than I can express. Perhaps you will oblige me. Provided you are able and disposed to oblige me, I should be pleased to be assured it is the skull of an Indian with no white blood in him.

"Mayhap your war chiefs may possess some such head which could be procured for me."

This letter was accompanied by one from my grandfather to his brother, dated Washington, Dec. 22d, 1820, in which he says: "I enclose with this a letter from my son Charles in Philadelphia. He is quite enthusiastic relatively to the sciences connected with his profession.

"He has four sons; his practice, in that wealthy and elegant city, is increasing, and I indulge a presentiment that he will do honor to his parentage and his name. If you can gratify his scientific wishes you will cheerfully do it." In a postscript he adds, "The inhabitants of Amsterdam Island are said to have very low foreheads—perhaps one inch between the eyebrow and the eye. To my good boy, who like me loves money less than knowledge, this object is interesting."

In 1831 he translated and published Velpeau's "Elementary Treatise on Midwifery," which was dedicated to Dr. James. The work must have been successful, since a second edition appeared in 1838.

The first independent work published by him was one entitled "The Philadelphia Practice of Midwifery."

It appeared in 1838, and was a small octavo of 370 pages. This must have had some success since it was exhausted in three years, as I find from the preface to a second edition, in the form of a large octavo of 408 pages, which was issued in 1842. The preface bears date December, 1841, and in it he says: "Three years ago this work was issued from the press . . . . In the space above mentioned, the work has been exhausted from the book shelves, and I have been invited by the bookseller and publisher to prepare a second edition." This work was, as he states in the preface, "An exposition of the most common views upon obstetric subjects, whether theoretical or practical, as held among my medical brethren in this city."

The publication of this work and of his translation of Velpeau's Treatise, showed conclusively that he had taken up obstetrics as his special branch of medicine, and though he attended as a general practitioner, and had a large business in that way, his main strength was given to the study, by observation and reading, of obstetrics.

His reputation as a practitioner, both of medicine and obstetrics, grew fast, so that by 1835 he had acquired such a position and income that he determined to remove to a more central part of the city. Accordingly he bought, about that time, a house in Chestnut Street above Tenth, south side, in the very centre of the business and fashion of the day, where he continued to live until 1850, and where he obtained all the practice he could attend to.

In 1841 he was elected to the post of Professor of Obstetrics and the Diseases of Women and Children, in the Jefferson Medical College of this city, entering that school with his friends Dr. Franklin Bache, Dr. J. K. Mitchell, and Dr. Mütter.

This appointment gave him the first opportunity of showing fully what was in him. He threw himself into the work with the greatest ardor. He studied every thing connected with his branch. He re-opened his Latin and Greek authors. He studied German, and read indefatigably in that language, until, without being at all a finished scholar in it, he was able to read with some ease the most important German obstetric authors of the day. He took great pleasure in his lectures during the first years that he occupied the chair. They were a constant and agreeable stimulus to his mind, and, being new ground for him, broke into the tedium of his daily routine work among the sick. Being thoroughly versed in all his subjects, and having a most active mind and lively imagination, which readily felt the stimulus of large classes and a sympathetic audience, he was roused to efforts which this new field alone served to bring forth, and to show to himself and to others what latent powers he had.

In the sixth year of his professorship he published the first independent work he had written since the Philadelphia Practice of Midwifery. This was an octavo volume of 670 pages, and was published by Lea & Blanchard in 1847. Its title was, "Woman, Her Diseases and Remedies." It was written in the form of letters to medical students, and it is one of the most original medical works of this country. It is based very largely on the practical knowledge of women's diseases he had acquired by personal experience, during the thirty years he had now been actively engaged in business in this city.

I doubt whether there is any American medical work which so clearly shows the character of the author as this. The style is peculiar and original. It is easy, flowing, graceful, and often eloquent, and there runs through the whole book a vein of sentiment, a thread of morality, in the form of appeals to the conscience and honor of the student, in his treatment of these diseases, which must strike every one who reads. There is in it a tone of easy familiarity with the subject, and with the reader, which is very agreeable. Its explanations are clear and distinct. The opinions expressed upon the nature and symptoms of the diseases referred to, and upon the methods of treatment, are full and positive. No man can doubt, as he reads, that the author has himself seen all that he has described, and that he has no doubts as to the propriety and correctness of the plans of treatment proposed.

In 1849 he issued the first edition of the work entitled, "Obstetrics, the Science and the Art," which was, in fact, a continuation of the Philadelphia Practice of Midwifery. This work, which was intended to be a treatise upon his special branch, contains a complete exposition of the anatomy and physiology of generation, a full description of pregnancy, and a full account of the process of childbirth in all its natural and preternatural aspects. It, like its predecessor, is eminently his own work. Though full of knowledge of all that had been done up to his time by domestic and foreign workers, by English, French, and Germans, and by the ancients as well as moderns, we see in it an amount of personal experience brought to bear upon any point of practice, which is seldom equalled. In the chapters on the physiology of generation he follows the best opinions of the day, but in discussing methods of treatment there is a constant reference to original observations, which demonstrates him to have been a man of great and most varied experience. The style here, as in the work on diseases of women, is quite original. He never hesitates to put a thing in his own way, is always ready, and often very attractive, in his descriptions of scenes witnessed by himself in the lying-in-room.

In 1850 he wrote a small work of 211 pages on certain diseases of children, and in 1854 a "Treatise on Acute and Chronic Diseases of the Neck of the Uterus." This was illustrated with 22 plates, colored and plain, and contained 116 pages. In 1854 he issued still another work, one on "Childbed Fevers." This last work contained 356 pages, and is written in the form of letters to his class. It is dedicated to his great friend, Dr. LaRoche, in writing to whom he refers to their "constant and loving friendship for more than twenty-five years."

In 1845 he translated a "Treatise on the Diseases and Special Hygiene of Females," by Colombat de L'Isère. This was a large, closely-printed octavo volume of 720 pages, and it, like the last work, was dedicated to Dr. LaRoche. A second edition was called for and issued in 1850.

Besides the preparation of the five original works I have just enumerated, he was obliged to revise several editions of his works. The first edition of the Letters on the Diseases of Women was published, as stated, in 1847. In 1850 a second edition, in 1854 a third, and in 1859 a fourth, were required, all of which were passed through the press under his own sole superintendence.

The work on Obstetrics, first published in 1849, passed into a second edition in 1852, a third in 1856, a fourth in 1863, and a fifth in 1867, and all this work was by himself alone.

In addition to these larger works he published some which, though of small size compared with treatises on any of the great branches of medicine, were large enough to require a good deal of time and thought in their preparation. In 1849 he printed, but did not publish, an essay of sixty-eight pages on the sporadic cholera, addressed to Dr. Sam. George Morton. In 1851 he wrote, for the Academy of Natural Sciences, of Philadelphia, a memoir of Sam. George Morton, M.D., of forty-eight pages. In 1853 he read before this body a biographical notice, of thirty-eight pages, of Daniel Drake, M.D., of Cincinnati.

These various works, all of which were written in the midst of the most arduous and fatiguing obstetrical and general medical practice, and whilst he was in the habit of lecturing four times a week during the winter lecture courses, exhibit, I think, a remarkable example of what the vital centres of the human machine can occasionally accomplish—I say occasionally accomplish, for I am convinced there are few men born into this world who can do in the way of work what my father did during these years.

But all this labor began at last to tell upon even his elastic frame. His health began to give way—not that he had any special disease of any special organ—he began to wear out. He still carried on for some years his practice and his studies and writing, but it was evident to us at home that the work was fast ceasing to be a pleasure, and becoming a very wearisomeness to the flesh. Though when abroad he was still the attentive, painstaking, interested physician—though at his desk he still kept up his lively style of writing, and his constant habit of reading—we at home began to see a change. There crept over him a despondency in regard to his own health. He began to complain of great fatigue, then of constant weariness, and, towards the last of his active life, of unmitigated and immitigable wretchedness. I doubt whether there be many forms of human suffering more distressing than the nervous disturbances brought about by long-continued overuse of the vital centres, such as professional and business men, and women with large families and deficient incomes, have to experience. And when, in spite of this low health, the subject must, or will, persist in working the exhausted frame, there can be nothing but acute pain, or a blasted reputation, to give rise to equal misery. The contention with the wearied body, the fight against morbid, involuntary fancies, the almost constant expectation of death coming ere long in some ghastly shape, the broken sleep, the disgusted appetite—all these things, and much more, did I see in my father for several years before he yielded to the cumulative proof that he must yield.

About 1856, when he was sixty-four years of age, he began to make serious preparations for retirement from active life, and with this end in view bought, after looking at several different localities, a spot of land of thirty-seven acres, to which I had the pleasure of directing him, in Delaware County, eighteen miles from the city. He bought of Mr. Mark Pennel, who thus became his next neighbor, and who, a farmer by birth, was one of the best and truest men I have ever met. He became one of my father's greatest friends in his latter years, and I will not let this occasion pass, without saying that his kindness and attention did much to make my father's residence at his little country-seat agreeable and happy.

Directly after purchasing these acres, which were located on the top and slope of a fine hill, with more than three-fourths of the land covered with a luxuriant growth of noble woods, he set to work to build himself a house. The house was modelled on Downing's Northern Farm-house. It was built of hard, dark, gray stone, taken out of his own land.

And now, with this new interest aroused, with a mind and conscience satisfied that the time for a rightful rest was near at hand, he began again to take some pleasure in life. How delightful were those days! He was forced to take half a day or a day, now and then, to see how his buildings progressed, and what pleasure to witness his interest and improving health under this new stimulus. His enthusiasm and poetry again woke up to activity, and he never tired of hearing and talking about this new comforter. His admiration of the site he had chosen, and of the building, as it rose upon the hitherto bare hill, it was delightful to hear. I recollect so well asking him once, upon his return to town after a short excursion to see the work done, "How does the house look?" "Look!" said he; "why, it looks like Windsor Castle." Asking him again, on another occasion, the same question, he replied: "Why, it looks like—like Chatsworth, by George!"

He built himself not only a house, but a barn and stable, a tenant-house, a spring-house, an ice-house, a work-shop, and all in the prettiest and most agreeable styles. And when all was finished, his houses and land had cost him but about fifteen or sixteen thousand dollars. He now sought a name for his new domain, and, amongst others, wished to call

2

it Paraclete, the Comforter; but my mother objected to what might seem at least an impropriety in the use of so holy a word, and he chose the Indian name of a small river in Connecticut, hard by which his forefathers had settled, and he called it Hamanassett.

When all was ready he sent my mother, with such of his children as could go, and my children, to pass the summer at the place; and in the summer months he would go down himself, returning to town, at first daily or every other day, to attend to such cases as he could not well cast off. After one of these visits he walked down the hill from his house, towards the railroad station, to return to town. My mother accompanied him to the gate, which she held open as he passed through, miserable and sad at leaving her and his country home. As he passed through, he turned and said, sadly, "Mary, I feel now as Adam must have felt when he left the garden of Eden, and the angel standing at the gate."

His health, though improved, continued feeble. He kept, from the time he bought Hamanassett, a garden record, in which he chronicled all the important events of his life—the planting of flowers, of garden vegetables, of crops, notes upon horticulture, garden farming, and all the events of a most interesting country life. I found, on looking over this diary, the following passage, of the date of Saturday, November 28th, 1857, evidently written in town: "I am suffering dreadfully with a most distressing gastrodynia, which assails me in exhausting paroxysms of pain, with a sense of weakness that makes me almost faint. . . . I sometimes almost doubt whether I *can* hold out to the end of the course (of lectures). I fear paralysis, like James Dewees, etc. If I can win to March, I *will* flee away from the distress—for it is distress—and be at peace at Ham (Hamanassett)." Again, Wednesday, Feb. 17th, 1858, he writes: "This day, 66 years ago, was I born, at St. George's, Bermuda, on the 17th Feb., 1792. I am now old and well stricken in years, and yet I labor diligently in my calling! How long!"

Soon after this time he carried into effect a purpose he had often talked about. He held that men ought to retire from public appointments, whilst they were still somewhat fresh in health. He thought that when they retained such positions to a late period of life, they sometimes lost the power of judging of their own fitness for duty, and also that decision of character which was necessary to induce them to lay down voluntarily their high positions. He had a fear lest he might defer his own decision as to the proper time for retiring, until he should lose the power or will to decide. So, after the course of 1859-60, he sent in his resignation to the trustees of the Jefferson Medical College, against, I believe, the wishes of his colleagues. But he was firm in his purpose and his successor was elected. This gentleman, after accepting the position, unfortunately fell into ill health and could not fulfil its duties. Towards the fall of 1860 my father was asked to give one more course, which he accordingly did, though against his will or wishes. At the close of that course he again resigned. I shall read to the college an extract from the minutes of the faculty, showing the action taken by his colleagues in this, his final resignation. It was sent to him, with a very kind note, by his old and fast friend, Dr. Dunglison, then dean of the college. The minute reads as follows: "The Faculty of the Jefferson Medical College of Philadelphia receive with deep sorrow the intelligence of the contemplated resignation of their distinguished colleague and friend, Professor Meigs.

"For a long time he had expressed a desire to withdraw from the incessant labors of the most arduous branch of an arduous profession. Still the Faculty had indulged the hope that it might be practicable for him to persist in his successful career of instructing others, which has been a labor of love with him, and to be content with abandoning, gradually or wholly, the practice of his profession.

"He has decided otherwise, however, and sighs for retirement, away from the busy scenes to which he has been accustomed in civic life; and all must admit, that if any one be entitled to dignified leisure it is he.

"The Faculty will part with him with intense and enduring regret. Never could any one have more closely applied himself to the execution of the responsible duties that have devolved upon him, and when sickness and sorrow have afflicted him, he was never absent from the amphitheatre at his accustomed hour without feeling keenly the privation.

"That he may reap every anticipated advantage from the course he has laid down for himself for the future, and may long be preserved to the cherished circle to which his continued existence is so important, and to the world of science, is the fervent wish of his colleagues.

Signed, "ROBLEY DUNGLISON,
"Dean of the Faculty."

In his garden record I find him writing the following words under date of Monday, 25th February, 1861: "This afternoon I delivered my last lecture at the Jefferson Medical College, and shall never more appear in public as a teacher of obstetricy, though I am to go on Wednesday at 4 P.M. to deliver an address of farewell to the class. I am surprised that this *finale* of my public life causes in me not the slightest excitement; I am simply very glad to get out of it. I am not mad with joy, but I am serenely cheerful at the prospect now before me of enjoying a little of the *libre arbitre* that I never yet did know."

After this time he did but little more professional work. He retired by degrees from all regular business, but still saw from time to time some of his old patients, who were anxious to consult him, or strangers who had come from a distance to have his opinion. It was very easy for me to see that he was entirely weary of all medical responsibilities. He lost even his taste for medical literature, and rarely looked into a medical book. I suppose the faculties employed in the study and practice of medicine for so many years were worn out by the severe toil they had undergone. In fact he had had too much of it, and even the recollection of the many anxieties he had passed through, and the excessive labor he had borne, made the past a painful retrospect. Certainly he had changed very much, for instead of enthusiasm there was disgust, and he turned gladly to literature for a rest, and for amusement and occupation.

I shall now give some account of his professional habits, then my own estimate of his character as a physician and medical writer and teacher, and finally read to you my son's description of his literary acquirements, and of the closing scenes of his life.

I have already begged the favorable consideration of the college for my, perhaps, too diffuse sketch of its departed member. Yet, I have found it impossible to say what I thought was due to his memory in fewer words, for he was a man of peculiar and original character, and one whose example in life may, I am sure, in most things, be fitly held up as a model for the future, whilst the lesson of his great success may serve to encourage others who shall have to begin life as he did, poor, unassisted, unknown, and with nothing but their own powers and high integrity to build upon.

Perhaps the most remarkable feature of his life was his wonderful activity. He was never idle. I never knew him to go to bed without a book in his hand. This is a literal fact. Unless ill, he always read after going to bed, no matter what the time of night might be. His manner of life for many years was the following : He had a large obstetric business and large general practice, neither of which were ever neglected. He was in the streets at work from nine in the morning until usually ten at night. In the middle of the day he had from half an hour to an hour for dinner, and in the evening, towards seven or eight o'clock, the same time for tea. His meals always taken in a hurry, and often interrupted by calls to the office, which, to the last, he would seldom refuse. Often up at night, often out all night, and snatching a few hours of sleep on a sofa or chair, for he rarely went to bed when attending a case of labor. When preparing his works for publication, it was very much his habit to take his manuscript with him when called to a case of labor, and to write busily in a neighboring room whilst the labor went on.

And yet, in spite of these great and continuous exertions, his mind was always active, bright and ready. He could sit down at any time, no matter how fatigued his body, and talk, write a letter, or work at any of his books, with an ease, rapidity, and relish which, to a man less gifted with such elastic vitality, may well seem astounding.

But not only did he possess and make use of this singular activity of the mental faculties. His moral sentiments and his emotional qualities were almost as remarkable. His temper was something to illustrate the profession to which he belonged. It was so sweet, so beneficent, so benevolent. Its patience was almost inexhaustible with the sick.

Dr. Wood says that Dr. Bache seemed unable to get angry. Though himself so absolutely upright, fair, and honest, even wrong-doing in another seemed unable to arouse anger in him. My father, on the contrary, though patient as a woman with the sick, could get very angry at times; vituperate in strong language what he condemned, and especially what he despised, but it was words, words. When the guilty came before him there was some under current of charity, of what Arthur Helps calls tolerance, some deep spring of tenderness towards weak humanity, which always led him to be gentle, considerate, forgiving. He hated to give pain to others, he loved to do good, and many poor weak human hearts that had yielded to the temptation to do wrong, found in him a wise mentor who could point rigidly to the way in which they should walk, and yet lend them large forgiveness.

At home he could not always control before the members of his own family the expression of the weariness and bodily exhaustion which, in the last ten years of his active life, so beset him. But, even then, it was only the complainings which he made in seeking for sympathy; it was never ill-temper. Did any one seek his professional advice in the office, all this weariness and lassitude were forgotten as he stepped across the threshold of the room devoted to the sick, and he became the patient, devoted physician, whose whole duty was to discover the cause of disease and the remedy. I think the triumph of duty over the morbid state of the nerves, determined by exhaustion, is one of the greatest triumphs of human nature. The patience of the mother amidst the wearing toil of a large family of children, especially when for the want of money she has to bear the whole burthen herself; the patience of an actor, who leaves a home of poverty and distress to display his histrionic powers before the public; the patience of some poor literary man, who toils, like Hood, amidst poverty and pain and ill health, to do his duty and sustain himself and his own against the assaults of penury, are great exhibitions of the bright side of human character; but I doubt whether any of these are as much worn down as the obstetrician in full career. His labor of each day is more constant and more exhausting. His nights are more sleepless. His duty calls into play all the great faculties of the mind and heart. He must use his senses to make his diagnosis, and he must use them often with all the abstraction his nature is capable of. He must use his powers of memory, comparison, and judgment to determine methods of treatment. In preternatural labor he must perform the most delicate operations, which are not only delicate, but difficult; which require a great length of time often for their performance, and during which performance all the senses of the physician are kept upon the very rack of expectancy.

But not only are judgment and the perceptive powers called into operation and kept, at such moments, at the highest tension of which the operator is capable. The emotional faculties, which often predominate in a character, and crowd into disgraceful and ruinous flight, on great emergencies, the nobler powers of the intellect and will, are here exposed to a degree of stimulation and disturbance, which will tax all the strength of the volition and self-control to keep them in due subjection and discipline. The accoucheur not only knows by his intelligence that the lives of his two patients, the mother and her child, may, and often do, depend upon his judgment and action, but he has his great responsibility there in bodily presence before him. There lies the body of that wife and mother which has been intrusted to his care; with her fate is entwined that of her husband, and, if she has other children, they are appealing to the physician that he forget nothing of his responsibility. How can he look upon that frail and sacred body, that casket of motherhood, that sweet embodiment of all the most exquisite emotions of human nature, and know and feel that it is intrusted to his care, and not have his body worn by the pressure upon it of such thoughts!

And, yet, my father, in spite of his constant exposure to all these causes of exhaustion, retained to the last of his professional life an unsurpassed sweetness of temper, and a patience which seems to me, even now, almost divine. Shall we not revere his memory for this, and hold him up as a model for those who are to follow him?

As a physician he was conspicuous by his devotion to his patients, his self-abnegation, his very high estimate of his responsibility to the sick, and his ever most conscientious discharge of every duty which could influence the progress of the case. These traits won for him from the public the greatest trust. Seeing him so deeply imbued with the importance of his work, and yet never hesitating to take prompt and decided action, because of his great confidence in his own judgment, the sick learned to confide in him with a fulness of faith and a sense of restfulness which, doubtless, had often much to do with their ultimate safety.

And then he was never mercenary. Born with a large æsthetic element in his nature, bred in the South, where he imbibed an unhealthy aversion to talking of money matters, hearing and seeing his father always exalting learning above money, he lived to be over fifty years of age before he seemed to awaken to the real value and uses of money. He could not face a verbal demand for his account without a kind of psychological tremor or nausea, and would creep or run away from it, if the patient would but let him. And if the asker, knowing this weakness of his, insisted, as sometimes he would, he never could screw his courage up to ask what he really deemed right, but would always choose for his standard some very low figure, which he was quite sure must seem moderate to the patient; for if there was one thing more odious to him than another, it was to have a patient whom he had benefited to even seem to think his charges exorbitant. Such an occurrence was gall and wormwood to him. When asked why he did not charge more according to his own estimate of the value of his services, his reply was, "He cannot pay me. My service was impayable. He ought to send me an honorarium." But besides this source of difficulty about charging, he was, as a habit, very careless, even reckless as to keeping any account of his daily visits. I knew him once not to enter a visit in his daily ledger for six weeks, and quite often he would make none for ten days. It was with him as I have heard it said it was with Dr. Chapman. But then Dr. Chapman had Mrs. Chapman, who was able to induce her husband to let her keep his books in some order. My mother, for a long time, assisted my father in the same manner, but finally he became so incorrigible that she had to give it up. The consequence of all this was, that when at last he did attempt to charge his visits, he had forgotten, I suspect, three-fourths. The occasion of this neglect was not altogether an æsthetic one. It was a bad habit, formed by his growing hatred to mere routine work or drudgery at home. Coming home tired and worn out, he could not resolve to set himself down to this mechanical work.

I cannot bring this sketch to a close without an attempt to show some of his opinions in regard to our common profession. His conception of what the physician ought to be, of the nature of his functions towards the sick, of his responsibility, of the breadth and depth of his work, were all of the highest order, and were so vigorously, eloquently, and forcibly pressed home upon the student, that I am sure no young man ever attended his courses without having his standard of what he should aim at elevated.

He always insisted upon a high standard of preparatory education. As early as 1829, in an oration delivered before the Philadelphia Medical Society, he said, " I shall state it as my opinion that a young man, destined to the study of medicine, should begin by obtaining a knowledge of the Latin and Greek, the French, German, and Italian languages. If the requisition be deemed exorbitant by any one, I am sure he will not continue long so to regard it, after having fairly set about their acquisition, particularly the three latter." He, on the same occasion, advised that he should study history, geography, voyages and travels, the varieties of the human race, and the effects produced on him by the climate, soil, food, manners, and political institutions of various countries.

In an introductory lecture of November, 1846, he says, "I acknowledge that I am an enthusiastic admirer of my profession. My speech declares it, and my whole past life is a perpetual proof of it. But I love that profession as a ministry, not as a trade. Can any human avocation have a stronger tendency to elevate and purify the mind, than that of the physician? What other? In what light shall he see the nature of man so clearly and so plainly?

" If you compare the tendency of these pursuits to raise the mind and the heart above the common level of humanity, with the similar tendencies of mathematics or pure physics, or the study of moral science, we find that they alike lift the contemplation to the throne and glory of God; that they alike show forth the littleness, vileness, and fruitlessness of man, his scope and endeavor. The mathematician and the astronomer in their investigations of the theory of the universe, in their detection of the laws of planetary and stellar motions, and in the farthest reaches of their thought as to the great cosmic influences and reactions discovered by reason's glance, by the power of numbers, or the magic of their glasses, cannot come nearer to a view of the power and wisdom and goodness of the Most High, than we in our studies of the laws and phenomena of the *life force* and of mind."

He ever taught in his lectures not only the absolute duty of the student to be always a student, in order that he might personally command the use of all that the observation and experience of the world were constantly discovering in the way of remedies and cures, but he also ever taught that there was in medicine a moral element, which did not enter so deeply into any other human vocation except that of the preacher. He always held that there was in the practice of medicine what he sometimes called a missionary element, a high flavor of charity which no man could, and no good man would, desire to escape from.

At the risk of being wearisome, I must make a few more extracts from his published lectures, as it seems to be only fitting to put on record in this biography, for the information of the future fellows of this institution, which is to last, I hope, for many long years to come, something of what he thought and published of our science in the 19th century.

In November, 1843, he spoke the following words to one of the large classes of Jefferson Medical College : " Your station is one of the most confidential character. Men, and women too, will open to you the secret griefs and shames that oppress them. Where is honor if you betray them ?

" You will be tempted to desert the path of duty under some pretence of doing good. Never do evil that good may come. Have a care lest you bring ruin on yourselves and discredit on all the brethren. The occasions to err are named legion. Be temperate, without reproach, charitable ; charity is a grace to all men,—to the physician, indispensable.

" The rewards of labor are sure, if not large. The fees of the physician are the honoraria—the honorable reward for intellectual labor. Take a just view of the nature and variety of this compensation. Values are determinate ; you cannot be paid with a price ; there is no tariff to be adjusted for health, nor an *ad valorem* for exemption from death. Hence, when, at a word and a glance, you save one from threatened dissolution, and he recognizes your service by a reward, it is the honorarium—the testimonial of his gratitude, not the measure of your service, for that is immeasurable. Now, when he presents you with a fee proportionate to his ability, you should accept it ; an humble one from the poor, and a richer one from the rich. It is convenient and proper to have some rule as a general means of direction, and for the information of the people ; but to measure all men by that rule is to be cruel as Procrustes. Must I say it ? Yes, our profession is not in general the road to wealth ; it is a sure one to competency. If it be riches you seek, make haste to seek them by some other action. . . . . No, your business in the world is one of charity. You must never turn a deaf ear to the cry of the poor. When you shall have become distinguished as practitioners, the poor will look upon you as well as the rich. A word! a kind word! oh, what a consolation to the distressed and humble poor from a rich and eminent physician! What a treasure of balm poured into the wounds of those who, alas! have few resources save in tears and silence !"

The preceding extracts will sufficiently show his views as to some of the most important ethics of the profession. I desire, also, to show forth one of his most distinctive traits—the peculiar regard he had for women, and especially the manner in which he referred to the sex in his daily teachings to his classes.

I think all will agree that it can be no easy matter so to deal with the subjects of obstetrical teaching, before a large class of young men, gathered from all parts of the country, as never, by word, phrase, or suggestion, to overstep the line of the purest modesty and delicacy; so to deal with all these delicate sexual matters, as ever to raise higher and higher the obedience of the classes to the highest law of manly devotion to the tenderer sex, ever to augment and to cause to glow with greater fervor these purest and best sentiments of the soul of man towards mother, sister, or wife. And yet my father did this with every class that listened to him, and the doing of it is one of the many acts of his life for which his memory ought to be honored and not forgotten.

In one of his introductory lectures, in referring to women, he says : " Every well-educated medical man ought to know something more of woman than is contained in the volumes of a medical library. Her history and literature, in all ages and countries, ought to be gathered together as the garlands with which to adorn his triumphant career as a physician; but these insignia of his power he can only gather by the careful and tasteful study of his subject among the rich stores of learning that are gained in the belles-lettres collections, whether archæological, mediæval, or modern. The medical man, surely, of all men, ought to be able to appreciate the influence of the sex in the social compact. But for the power of that influence, which of you would doubt the rapid relapse of society into the violence and chaos of the earliest barbarism ?

" Are you not aware that the elegance and the polish of the Christian nations are due to the presence of the sex in society, not in the zenana ? Do you not perceive that music, painting, poetry, and the arts of elegance, luxury, fashion (that potent spell), are of *her*, and through *her*, and in *her?* Versailles and Marly and the Trianons had never been built for men. The loom blends and sets forth the dyes that add richer reflections to *her* bloom ; the wheel flies for polishing the diamond that is to flash in impotent rivalry before her eyes. Sea and land are ransacked of their treasures for her ; and the very air yields its egrets, and marabouts, and paradise birds, that may add piquancy to her style, and grace to her gesture. Even literature and the sciences are in good measure due to her patronage and approbation, which is the motive power to all manly endeavor. This is true, since, but for her approving smile, and her rewarding caress, what is there should stir man from the sole, the dire, the unremitted compulsion to act that he may live ? With woman for his companion, he acts not only that he may live, but that he may live like a Christian and like a gentleman."

Again he says : " The female is naturally religious. Hers is a pious mind. Her confiding mind leads her more readily than man to accept the proffered grace of the Gospel. If an undevout astronomer is mad, what shall we say of an irreligious woman ? See how the temples of the Christian worship are filled with women. . . . . It is not until she comes beside him, in view of the people, that man ceases to be barbarous, and cruel, and ignorant.

" She spreads abroad the light of civilization and improvement as soon as she issues from the prison of the harem or zenana, to live with him in the parlor. Who made us human ? Whose were the hands that led us to kneel down, and whose the lips that taught our infant voices the earliest invocations to Heaven ?"

I have already adverted to some of his qualities as a lecturer. It is very eulogistic to say what I am about to say, and coming from me it may seem to be a mere filial over-estimate. I thought him, during the term of his activity in Jefferson Medical College, one of the very best and most admirable lecturers I had ever heard. And now, when I look back, since his death, at his lecture-room, and recall the power he exerted over his classes, and the memories of those days, I hold to my judgment.

If the estimate we are to put upon the value of a teacher is to be made from a consideration of what he effected, we must place him very high. When he first appeared upon the scene, I am quite sure that the classes of young men then coming to Philadelphia for medical learning, thought little of the importance and dignity of obstetrics, in comparison with the other practical branches, medicine and surgery. Many brought with them the old and vulgar prejudices that midwifery, as it was then usually called, was an old woman's kind of business, and that men should mingle with it only because they could not help themselves, and under a kind of protest. But my father soon changed this feeling, and made it one of the favorite branches of study in the college, and this, not only by demonstrating its great intrinsic importance to the public, but he raised it to a high dignity of its own by his constant portraitures of the tragic scenes through which the accoucheur had to wend his way ; by showing the heavy and anxious personal responsibility of the obstetric practitioner, and by throwing around it an atmosphere of romance and tenderness towards the sex, which touched even the rudest student, and awakened in his heart an interest and respect for this branch of medicine, which he had never dreamed of, until its true tints were held up before him so bright and clear that he could not fail to see them.

I have never heard an oral medical teacher who could so cause to flash before the mind of the student a true picture of the life scenes through which he was destined to pass—make him see, as it were, and prepare himself to act, in the crises and dangers and terrors of actual practice. When he described the attack of puerperal convulsions in some young and worshipped wife ; when he placed before us a woman fainting, dying perhaps, of uterine hemorrhage, or when he painted in touching words what he called the hysteroids of childbed fever, there was no man who did not see the future that lay before him, for was not this an artist picturing for us what he had himself so often seen ? And his power of vivid description made most welcome his minute and accurate explanations of the proper treatment to be pursued on all these occasions. And he could drive home upon his listeners a clear and lasting recollection of his plans of treatment, for he had a very distinct understanding of his own opinions ; he had no hesitations, no doubts as to what ought to be done on all occasions demanding the interference of the accoucheur. He would state distinct and positive rules, thus and so, and then iterate and reiterate in varying language—strike one blow, then another, pause to make an illustration, and return to fasten and clinch all that he had previously said. He was never tedious, for he was full of his subject, knew all that had been learned in regard to it, and through his long and busy practical life, had himself seen, over and over again, everything nearly that could happen in the lying-in-room. He was enthusiastic as to its importance to society, as to its high dignity as a human calling, and with a fine poetic element which was specially his, threw over it, and around it, and twined into it, with every medical law he laid down, that halo of love and tenderness and pity for women, which is inherent in all men, is as old as the race, and is to last as long as the race is to last.

And now, gentlemen, having finished what I had to say of the medical part of my father's life, I shall let my son describe his literary acquirements, and portray his inner character as it appeared to those who dwelt with him by his own hearthstone. He shall also describe for us his latter days. He has done this with a tenderness and truthfulness which I could not equal, and so we will commit to the archives of the college this sketch of one of our departed fellows, whose life was surely one of busy endeavor in good works not often excelled.

My son writes as follows :—

Nothing was so peculiarly his as the varied learning he began with the first dawn of reason to acquire. It is not at all wonderful that fellows of colleges in England, or industrious Germans, who have set apart their lives to fathom all the lore of time, should become learned; but that a man upon whom, not learning, but a harassing profession, had the first claim, that he should reach such a height of erudition, is truly a sight rare to behold. The natural love of ease, that is common to all men, was well nigh extinguished in my grandfather, and the only ease he knew, was that which noble natures feel when they have spent their high parts for the furtherance of the right.

But that this may not be thought the idle vaunt of family affection, I will mention a few of the widely different books that gave him the greatest pleasure, and thus any one may see how fertile a mind was his, that could take in the excellences of each of these opposite works without prejudice or damage to the others. First, then, all who knew him will remember that the book he loved most dearly was a treatise on the races of men by the Count de Gobineau. In these learned volumes my grandfather became wrapt up through and through, and saturated with the overflowing stream of their wisdom. As the years rolled on he never grew weary of the oft-told story of the first races of man, how they came from the hot marshes in the middle of Asia, and nourished themselves out of bone vessels which they scattered along the way, that generations to come might dig them up and unravel the story of their pre-historic hardships. And it was to him like the lifting of a curtain when he read how the simple-minded people, after unnumbered disasters, came at length to the Caucasus and went through the gates of Europe, where they spread themselves abroad and became slowly civilized by time, the great ameliorator of all things. My grandfather always put himself among the Aryan or noble race, and he liked to discover in his grandchildren the unmistakable marks of the Aryan outline as given by Gobineau. The prosperity of our country, and the rapid strides with which it has sprung up to greatness, were by him referred to the weight of Aryan blood in our veins; and, when our war was over and peace restored, his chief sonree of disgust was the backsliding which he foresaw from the terrible commingling of the nations.

He had such a delight in M. de Gobineau's writings that he began a correspondence with him when the Count was the French minister at Athens, and kept it up until the time of his death. And the last labor of his life was to translate a novel of his called "L'Abbaye de Typhaines."

A work that he read very much in his active life was the great treatise of Oken; he often trod wonderingly amid the luxuriant subtleties of German dialectics; and he was filled with awe and delight when he saw the jumps, antics, and drolleries that the human mind can perform when put to it.

Then it amused him greatly to read the quaint absurdities of the middle ages. He liked to hear about the wild ways of those boyish knights and jolly priests. Even the luxuriant folly and richness of iniquity that abounded in them gave him a sort of cold comfort, for he was a devout believer in the vanity of all things and the foolishness of this life. And, when he consulted those old landmarks and monuments of folly, he found that he was right. I think it was chiefly from Tallemant des Réaux that he drew those grotesque stories about the devil which he told in such an amusing way. Thus my grandfather, tired of the earth, and counting the days to his release, read these works and read them again, because he felt that the world was very evil; and this was a proof of it, showing him that his desire to be gone, and his disapproval of earthly things, were not in vain.

From Tallemant des Réaux he often went in an instant over the great gulf that lies between diabolical legends and Ritter's knowledge of the earth. He had very spiritual views about the power of evil, and no doubt he shared the common wonder of philosophers how a moral God can allow the existence of evil, but he was never so foolish as to dispute that it was so; for, with eyes as keen and fearful as the simple and pious who died hundreds of years ago, he saw the spirit of wrong in every bush, and discerned his marks in the child that was not yet weaned.

He was always thankful to any one who could tell him something about the dimly known kingdom of Persia, locked up in its barbarism by insuperable barriers of the elements. He loved to read about it because it was near the source whence issued the first stream of nations. I think he would have been sorry to see this labyrinthine web of Persia unwoven, so delicious to him was its slow disentanglement. In his meditations on the earth, as on all other things, he did not busy himself on the profound and unsearchable matters alone, but he took a child's delight in the pleasant tales current in Persia about the sweetness of their instruments of music, which rivalled Orpheus in giving a graceful motion to the cows and clumsy animals, and took away from the camels their thirst, satisfying them with music, instead of running water. The book from which he learned the most about Persia was, as usual, one of Gobineau's.

When all else failed him he used to go back confidently to a book that he must have known by heart many years before his death, a history of Gnosticism. This he liked, no doubt, for the same reason that he liked the legends of the knightly ages, because they gave him an insight into the corners and hiding-places of the mind, the loop-holes and crannies where it can get out. There is assuredly a sad consolation in hearing about the shoals and quicksands which the human reason has passed, and in counting the number of times that it has deviated from the true path;

for it teaches us that, if we fall, it is no disgrace, since our wise ancestors have fallen before us.

There can be few men in active professions in this country now who can show a small part of the learning that was my grandfather's, for he was thoroughly well versed in all the great histories of the old and new writers—Livy and Sallust, Thucydides, Guicciardini, and Gibbon—he knew them all. The ways of science were not hidden from him. The scant shreds of mystery that have been picked up in Egypt, the dark and nonsensical beginnings of the Greeks, the dreary wilderness of the Arabians, and the copious fields of natural magic that abounded in the middle ages, the great revolution planned by Bacon, the discoveries wrought by Newton, and the further unveiling and prying into the secrets of nature that has gone on in our own time, all were open to him, and he saw the worth of each of them. He might almost take into his mouth Manfred's words :—

> " Philosophy and science, and the springs
> Of wonder, and the wisdom of the world,
> I have assayed."

He had crowded together a vast mass of knowledge, of which the disorder in his library was symbolical. This was a very paradise of confusion, and the spirit of disorder there ruled over all. Here were three bookcases, whose arrangement was like that of the night before the creation. There was an Italian Bible of the sixteenth century almost squeezed to death between two fat volumes of obstetrics ; and of the complete works of Cicero there were generally two or three volumes on a piano stool for the children to sit on. The mantelpiece was in a yet more uncultivated state than the book-shelves. The centre-piece was commonly a tin canister of hunkidora tobacco, looming up from a waste of empty matchboxes, two or three half-finished busts of General Grant, and some scissors for pruning the trees, all of which had a tendency to be brought together by the lumps of bees-wax that were scattered about. From this disordered wild, lying on a cushion, which the dogs had almost torn to pieces, and with Humboldt's Cosmos staring him in the face, he was wont to declaim to his grandchildren upon the incalculable advantages of order, and the keen pleasure it gave him to see everything in its place.

The terrors and distresses of our war bore so heavily upon him that he began at this time to show that he was an old man, and to impress us more with the sense of his age than he had ever done before. His grandchildren learned to keep themselves out of sight, lest they might be taken away from their sports, and sent to a neighboring house, or to meet the arrival of a train, that they might glean some bits of intelligence about the movements of the great army. And woe to him who was so thoughtless as to visit Hamanassett without a full budget of news; the more newspapers, the more welcome the guest, and the eager consultation of the war-columns often took precedence of the reception of the new comer. And, then, without reading a word, my grandfather used to throw them all down, and say they gave him such an agony of distress that he could not read them.

It is no wonder that any unusual noise should have troubled him, as he sat pensive and distressed upon his lonely hill. The hoarse screech of the locomotive was intolerable to him. So he made an agreement with the conductor of the train that, if any battle of disastrous end should be known in the city, he should give two whistles with his engine, but for a successful contest he should whistle twice as often.

Besides the sorrows that were given him by each defeat or loss of blood suffered by our arms, my grandfather went through a very sore affliction in the loss of a grandson,[1] who was his favorite and pride among all his descendants in the third generation. It was always an aim of my grandfather to advance the name of which he was the oldest bearer in the place where we live. And from his earliest childhood, high actions and noble exploits were looked for at the hands of this grandson. My grandfather, at least, thought himself endowed with a spirit of prophecy, for he expected his own death with no greater certitude than did he look for the prowess and renown of this grandson in after years. But alas ! his prophetic utterances of the future were brought to nought, and his hopes dashe   by the last mournful event, even by the descent of the Ange   ath upon the lusty youth that he had so dearly loved. Fearless   from his boyhood, and taken away from his studies at the Military Academy of West Point, to fight in one of the most luckless engagements of our war, where he bore so brave a part that he received the thanks of several commanders of important posts, and had his gallant conduct cheered by the whole of his fellows in arms ; this generous youth was struck down in an instant, and killed, by one of the partisans of the day. It was one of those dread events, full of mystery, that strike terror into the stoutest heart. This good young man, who knew not a sensation of fear, and from whom vicious actions and fraud were far off, was cut down in the twinkling of an eye. He was deprived of fame, and his shining qualities, and the precious jewels of learning with which he had adorned them, were buried in the earth. His country lost the profitable harvest that she might have reaped from his high parts, and his unoffending parents drooped beneath their heavy punishment.

When Goëthe heard of the great earthquake at Lisbon, where sixty thousand men were killed in sixty minutes, he lost the little trust in Providence that he ever had. But my grandfather's mind rose faithful still, and strong, above the dreadful sorrow ; and I never could see that the death of his favorite in the least shook his belief in the benevolent government of the world. But a more terrible trial than this was preparing for him ; the Angel of Death had not gone back to his abode among the spirits, but was fluttering about still, and waiting only to come again and afflict yet more grievously the gray, venerable state of my grandfather. His grandson had been seven months in the grave, and the keenness of his grief for him had begun to lose its edge, when my grandmother, having reached the allotted period of her life, was called to her long home.

She was not my grandfather's better half; she was his whole earthly existence, without whom he desired not to live. The world, that had long been imbittered to him, became irksome to him now, and he would gladly have left it. But this was not to be, and he stayed with us four years more, slowly pining away in grief both of soul and body. For at the end of his life he suffered untold distresses with a bodily infirmity that took away his peace when he was able to console himself for the loss of his sweet partner. Many a long year he had borne in silence an unceasing pain from some disorder in a bone of his leg. But as he was a man who shrank from any show of weakness or being disabled, it was

[1] Lieutenant John R. Meigs, son of General Montgomery C. Meigs.

his habit to tend this sore member alone, and he ever refused to show it
to any one, though by consulting a learned physician he might have saved
himself some measure of pain.

Rent by these two conflicting woes, he was the most amiable and the
gentlest of men, and to the memory of his sons and daughters these days
of misery are among the enjoyablest of his life, for in them he showed
the beautiful contentedness of his spirit, and the stern self-denial with
which he set his own mishaps aside.

Perhaps his stoutness in resisting, and his bravery, were wasted; perhaps he did not economize them as he ought, but let such noble qualities
have their due, all honor let them have wherever they appear.

It is possible oftentimes for a mind free from taint to conquer the cries
and lamentations of the body; for men, the more learned and the wiser
they become, do acquire a certain contempt for the material parts of them,
but the cries of the spirit cannot be set aside. The body may be crushed
down and beaten, but the spirit " groaneth and travaileth in pain."

My grandfather, besides the bodily pain that he was ever suffering under,
and the loss of the beloved wife who had never left him for fifty years,
had to leave the shrubbery and fruit trees that he had used to tend, and
he must come back to this uninviting town, whose hot red bricks and
monotonous lanes he had long ago learned to hate, for he never thought
of them but with the distressed women and dying children that he had
known as their inmates. Cooped up in a second-story room, he pined
for the peace and quietude of his pleasant home at Hamanassett. And
each year he frightened his friends and neighbors by threatening to leave
the ugly town, and find a little happiness in the fields alone.

Surely, sudden death is to the untutored soul a thing much to be
dreaded. It is the prayer of the whole creation to be delivered from
sudden death. Most of us would do all that we could to ward it off, and
we should have an untranquil spirit if we knew that we were to be put
out like a candle in the twinkling of an eye, without a moment of decay
to warn us of the end. But to my grandfather the termination of his life
was but "a quiet night and an end of his toils." There was only a little
left of his mortal self; his flesh and bones were all out of joint, and he
pined for dissolution. Without pretence, or making a parade of his fear-
lessness of death, he looked to it as a kind messenger that would relieve
him of many a burden. He now redoubled his studies, and his mind was
never so young and so vigorous as when his body was fast wearing out.
The earthly and the spiritual were in a divine warfare, and while his flesh
ached and his bones were poured out like wax, his soul triumphed over
them, sending forth the sparks from its unabated lustre. All of him that
could die was now near its end, but the soul was laughing, and proud of
its own strength, and he might have been with us now, had not the heavy
chains of matter dragged him down.

At this time the consolations of philosophy, which he drank in with
such zest, were chiefly studies upon the races of men, and the curious re-
ligions they had built up for themselves by their unaided reason ; systems
which, though they be doomed to fall, do yet in a wonderful way set forth
the glory of us, who are the highest work of creation ; he often busied
himself, too, in studies upon the difference of races, and the results of
their mixing with one another. Thus, by a beautiful inconsistency, while
he was sinking beneath the weight of years, and the breath well nigh gone
out of him, his greatest solace was to dwell upon the glories of the human

race, and the excellence of the strength of which he was soon to have no
more in this world.

But his state in his latter days was not altogether an unhappy one.
He was full of misery, and rent with the shame which his proud nature
could not but feel, when it saw itself prostrate and begging help from
the children he had aided at their birth; but, then, he had the comfort-
ing remembrance that he had not wasted the trust committed to him,
and the enviable knowledge that rose up triumphant against his modesty,
and told him that he had accomplished well his work on earth.

It is the habit of some good men steadfastly to contemplate their
death at certain times; yet this, so far as we know, was never a part of
my grandfather's daily life, though it is an ennobling exercise, tending to
lift us above the poor things of the earth, and teaching us to perform
with honor to ourselves, and profit to others, the last part we shall ever
have to play in the world.

Therefore, my grandfather, though the contemplation of death was not
an office which he went through daily according to rule, yet by no means
neglected to look forward to his separation from the body with such devotion and awe, such humility and trustfulness as was becoming. And it is
probable that he thought of it much oftener than those about him were
aware of. When he felt more than commonly bowed down with pain, and
when his grandchildren, who were his most frequent companions, were
drawn off to something else, then no doubt he bent his thoughts on death.

He spent many hours of each day in meditation, and often passed
sleepless nights, when the image of death must have been present to him,
but he never came to any further conclusion than that he wanted to be
taken away from this scene of vanity. Not once in his whole life did I
ever know him to harbor a black thought about the world to come; or,
still worse, one of those terrible doubts whether there be any world to
come.

It is often said that those about to die have a secret foreshadowing of
their end; so none of us pass away all at once, but each one of us has a
warning, more or less clear, of what is at hand. But, if my grandfather's
outward signs and speech could be taken for indications of what passed
within, no such foreknowledge was ever vouchsafed to him, except the
constant wish that he had to die, and his state of being always ready for
it. Two days before his death he had two of his sons from distant parts
of the country staying in his house, and he presided at the Sunday dinner with all his usual sprightliness and grace.

One bright morning in the summer, when all nature was full of life, he
was found dead in his bed, having passed away quietly and apparently
with so little knowledge of his approaching death that, up to the time
when he went to sleep, he was employed about his common avocations;
and there was a volume of Pythagoras on his shelf, with other works of
philosophy. As it was his consolation to be gone, so was it ours that
he went without pain. He died just as he had always wished to die,
and passed peacefully away in the midst of a tranquil sleep on the 22d
of June, 1869, at the age of 77 years.